THE DAY I FOUND A WORMHOLE AT THE BOTTOM OF THE GARDEN

TOM McLAUGHLIN

WALKER
BOOKS

First published in Great Britain 2019 by Walker Books Ltd
87 Vauxhall Walk, London SE11 5HJ

2 4 6 8 10 9 7 5 3 1

Text and illustrations © 2019 Tom McLaughlin
Cover design © 2019 Walker Books Ltd

The right of Tom McLaughlin to be identified as author/illustrator of this work has been asserted by him in accordance with the Copyright, Designs and Patents Act 1988

This book has been typeset in Stempel Schneidler

Printed and bound by CPI Group (UK) Ltd, Croydon CR0 4YY

British Library Cataloguing in Publication Data:
a catalogue record for this book is available from the British Library

ISBN 978-1-4063-7581-7

www.walker.co.uk

THE DAY I FOUND A WORMHOLE AT THE BOTTOM OF THE GARDEN

For the coffee farmers of the world, without whom I wouldn't have been able to finish this book.

1 p.m.

Can you remember the best day of your life? Perhaps it was when you bought a tube of Fruit Pastilles and discovered that the entire packet was made up of green ones. Maybe it was the day it snowed and your school was one of the ones that closed. Or maybe it was the day your school was closed and you bought a packet of Fruit Pastilles to celebrate and discovered that they were all green.

Billy can remember his best day. It was the occasion of his ninth birthday; the day that he got a metal detector from his nan. It combined his two favourite things in the world: gadgets and digging massive great holes. It was like having his very own giant lucky-dip box to play with. Who knew what treasure he might find! Would it be an ancient chest of gold coins hidden by a bearded pirate? Or a bejewelled sword that once belonged to an old forgotten king? Or even a cursed bejewelled sword that once belonged to a cursed king? Things in the olden days always had curses.

Since his birthday, Billy had explored nearly every inch of the garden – making his parents' lawn holier than a piece of Swiss cheese – and, so far, he'd found several ring pulls from cans of fizzy pop and a coin dating back to the mid 90s! But now, Billy needed a new place to explore; uncharted territory … a land full of possibilities. As he lay on his bed, enjoying a post-lunch power-nap, he was suddenly struck by an idea.

"THAT'S IT!"

Billy yelled out with excitement.

As if on cue, Shakespeare jumped on the bed and licked Billy's eyelids. Shakespeare was Billy's French bulldog; he had a very small brain and very big ears and was often mistaken for an angry rabbit.

"No, down boy, please … yuk! Stop licking my eyes … it's gross! Oh, your breath!" Billy cried out. "Some dogs fetch their owner's slippers, you know." Billy sat up in bed, wiped the slime from his eyeballs and contemplated his plan.

There was one place that he hadn't explored, somewhere no one ever went … the bottom of the garden. It was just past the deadly blackberry bush and its many spikes of doom, over the old compost heap, through the weird-smelling boggy bit and next to the abandoned shed. Mum and Dad called it the "icky place" and Billy had been frightened of it for as long as he could remember; it was dark, damp and scary-looking, like some sort of boggy nightmare. But now he was older and able to put his fears aside all in the name of history and digging stuff up. Today was going to be the perfect day for it, Billy thought checking his watch, because today…

DING DONG!

The doorbell rang out.

"Nan's here." Billy smiled. "Perfect timing!"

"Bill—y!" his mum shouted.

Billy hopped off the bed, gave Shakespeare a wink and bounded down the stairs. Billy lived in a small, uninteresting house in Clapham that had a neat front garden and a rather holey back garden. It was down a short cul-de-sac – the sort of place where people twitched their curtains when a new car appeared in the street and where there were lots of signs that said:

NO BALL GAMES

above tiny patches of grass, as if an entire gang of kids could somehow use it to play the world's smallest game of football. Billy landed at the bottom of the stairs and gave his nan a hug. She was here to babysit.

"Hello, lad," Nan said and started to shuffle into the living room.

"Right," Mum said and turned to Billy. "You know what to do. It's the usual routine. Not too much TV, don't eat lots of sweets and no, I repeat, no dancing on the tables again!"

"Don't worry, I'll look after her," Billy said. Sometimes it felt like he was the babysitter, not the other way round.

"I am capable of looking after my grandson, you know!" Nan said gruffly to Mum. "The table-dancing was a one-off."

"I don't want to talk about Skittle-gate." Mum glared at them both. "Not again."

"We'll be fine," Billy said calmly. Mum had no idea of the dastardly plans that were being hatched inside his brain.

"Look, I made you some rock buns, lad.
I know they're your favourite," Nan said,
reaching into her handbag – not into a
cake box, or a napkin, but into her actual
handbag – and taking out a cake that
must have been sloshing around with her
keys and dirty change. She handed it to
Billy and beamed at him.

When he was five, Billy had made the mistake of saying he liked them, which Nan had taken to heart, and now claimed they were his favourite. Billy always tried to eat them, but the darn things were so hard that he'd never got past the outer crust. It was like giving a hamster a coconut and telling him to tuck in. Billy assumed that Nan had misread the recipe and used real rocks to make them, rather than, say, flour and eggs and actual edible stuff.

A few years ago, someone had tried to pinch Nan's handbag – an awful thing to do to an old lady. But Nan being Nan, and thinking on her feet, reached into her bag during the kerfuffle, grabbed the first thing that came to hand – a rock cake – and cracked it over

the attacker's head. It knocked him clean out and Nan became a hero; she even appeared in the local paper with a picture of her holding a rock cake like it was a hand grenade. Since then, she never left home without a cake, or the recipe for that matter.

"Thanks, Nan." Billy smiled and pretended to take a bite. "Yummy. So very firm and not like these modern cakes that melt in your mouth." He grinned. Mum gave Billy a knowing look.

"Right, son," Mum said, "we're off shopping. Your birthday isn't too far away and we have lots of other things to get done, so we'll be gone for a few hours. But remember, any mischief and Nan will call us and we'll be back here straight away!"

Billy nodded, knowing that this was basically a lie. Yes, there was a phone in the house, but Nan had no idea how to use it. Billy had seen her pointing it at the TV not so long ago to try and get the snooker on BBC Two.

"Of course, Mum."

"Don't forget your homework, it's history, isn't it? You have to write about meeting a historical figure. I know creative writing isn't your bag, but please try and make an effort. So, as soon as we're gone, crack on with it. Me and your dad … where is he? Steve!" Mum yelled. "Anyway, we'll be back as quick as we can … STEVE!"

"Coming…" Dad sighed. The prospect of missing the football to go shopping was not an appealing one for him.

"Are you ready? Do you have everything?" Mum asked.

"Yes, keys and … well, that's it, right?" Dad said.

"Let's go!" Mum said with the steely look of a general about to send her troops into war.

The door slammed, an engine revved and the two were gone, off for an afternoon of wandering around the shopping centre and trying not to fall out with each other. Billy smiled and clapped his hands. Now it was time for the real plan. Time to send Nan to sleep for a few hours while he got on with some proper exploring.

"This way, Nan. What about a nice cup of tea?" Billy said. "Nice and milky with five sugars?" He smiled. "Let me get your special cushion. Look what I recorded for you on the digi box…"

"Is it my show?" Nan said gleefully, settling into a chair. "Did you record them on the tape player?"

"Yep, fifteen hours of *Antiques Roadshow*. The first episode is live from Windsor Castle," Billy said putting a cushion behind her. He loved the understanding they had. Nan would fall asleep pretty much as soon as she arrived and Billy would be left to his own devices – mainly digging up the back garden. He hit play and – three … two … one – she was out for the count.

There was something about the sight and sound of well-to-do gentlemen in bow ties pointing at old clocks that overwhelmed her. Perhaps it reminded her of simpler times, but whatever the reason, the result was the same. She was asleep, and she would stay asleep as long as the TV was on.

Let the fun begin.

2 p.m.

Billy rushed upstairs and opened his wardrobe. "I need a hat ... explorers always wear some kind of headgear." He looked at his vast collection of firemen's hats, trilbies and top hats. "Hmm ... these might be a little over the top," he murmured. Then he spotted his good, sturdy baseball cap and grabbed it. "Perfect," he said, pulling the cap down over his curly hair.

Billy opened the next door along, took a deep breath and beamed with delight as he looked at his metal detector glinting in the sun. He could almost hear the choir singing as he pulled it out and held it aloft like it was a medieval sword. "Hello, Bess," he said sweetly. Billy didn't know if it was the done thing or not to name one's own metal detector, but he didn't care. "Billy and Bess on another metal-detecting adventure," sounded good to him. Now all he needed was his trusty steed.

"Shakespeare!" Billy yelled. There was a sound of footsteps scrabbling up the stairs, a door being opened and a *woof* of disappointment.

"Wrong room, Shakespeare!" Billy shouted.

"YOU'RE IN THE BATHROOM! I'M IN MY BEDROOM!"

Shakespeare, for all his large ears, seemed to have a terrible sense of hearing. Finally, he ran into the right room and bounded up to Billy, his tail wagging eagerly.

"Right, lad, here's the plan, we're going to the bottom of the garden, further than any human has gone for many a moon. There we will detect like never before. Are we going to be put off by a few stinky weeds and creepy-crawlies? No! Today is the day. Today we will return from the land beyond the compost heap with untold treasure. Are you ready?" Billy asked.

Shakespeare stared at Billy with his tongue hanging out and did a small bottom-squeak.

PRUUUUP

"My feelings exactly, but we've got to be brave. Go where others fear to tread... Now, where did I put my big wellies?"

Five minutes later, Billy, Bess and Shakespeare were ready. Billy fired up Bess and waved her around the living room next to Nan. Every time it went near her false teeth, the metal detector whistled. The test achieved two things: checking Bess was working and making sure Nan was asleep. It was a thumbs-up for both. It was on.

Wrrrreeeeewwwwiiiii

Billy grabbed an apple for a mid-hike snack and plodded through the living room towards the patio doors. He looked like an astronaut walking on the moon; his wellies rippled and warbled with every step. They were Dad's old ones, but with five pairs of socks, they just about fitted Billy. The wellies were perfect for keeping out scuttley, bitey creatures that might be lurking at the bottom of the garden.

Billy opened the back door and searched around the patio for any equipment that he might need for his treasure hunt. He found a small trowel and fork, some rope and a pair of thick gardening gloves. Billy stuffed them into his backpack and headed down the path, passing the neat flowers and grass. It must have been his imagination, but as he approached the end of the garden, the sun disappeared and the wind began to swirl around. Shakespeare started whimpering. Billy stopped, took a breath and headed for the place beyond the blackberry bush. Between the thorns and half-eaten fruit, he could just make out what used to be a path.

"Right, lad, time to use the rope!" Billy said to Shakespeare. He pulled it out of his backpack, made a loop and threw the rope over the bush, tying it back so that he could get past the spikes of doom. "Phase one complete," Billy said triumphantly. Was it time to munch the apple? He was a bit peckish, but he had only been exploring for twenty seconds. Maybe save it for later.

Billy and Shakespeare slowly crept around the old compost heap until they reached the boggy bit that smelt really bad. Beneath the tall grasses, Billy could see the old shed. This was where he would start looking. He carefully stepped over the boggy patch and used the trowel to hack the tallest of the grass away. Shakespeare sat on a large rock near the shed, looking most put out that he was roughing it in

a smelly wilderness. Once he had cleared the area, Billy put his headphones on, fired up Bess and waved her close to the ground.

"Here we go! There's buried treasure near by. I can feel it! The first question isn't will I find anything, but when and what? The second is, what will I spend all that money on?" What to spend the money on was what kept Billy going – it was the thing that made him carry

on looking in the wind and rain, when he could have been inside drinking tea and eating warm buttered toast. Some can go a lifetime looking and never find anything more than a few pence, but Billy knew that one day soon he would hit the jackpot.

"I think I've finalized my top five things that I want to buy when I become a millionaire," Billy said to Shakespeare, who yawned and let out another bottom-squeaker. "Number one: someone to do all my homework for me. Although, depending on how rich I get, maybe I could just buy the school and turn it into a sweet shop or something. Number two: a vintage top hat, a really tall and shiny one that actually fits. None of the

grown-up ones fit my head and I want a proper kids' one made. Number three: a robot butler. Number four would be a time machine. I know they don't actually exist, but I'm sure if I paid someone enough, they'd invent one for me. What do you think, boy?" Billy said, looking over at Shakespeare, who was almost asleep by now. Billy sighed. "Maybe number five should be I'll buy a cat—"

WEEEeeerrrrEEEEEEEIIIIIIIiiiii!

The metal detector whirred into life. He looked down and, without taking his eyes off the patch of soggy grass, he slowly put Bess down. He reached into his backpack, grabbed his gloves and the trowel and began to dig very carefully. Metal-detecting was a precise business – whatever was down there might be delicate. Billy scooped away the earth, until there was a tinkling sound as the metal of the trowel hit something hard. He used his hands for the next bit, picking away at the soil until he felt something jagged under his glove. He grinned as he pulled the object from the ground.

"Can it be?!" Billy beamed with delight. "I think it is, yes!" he yelled, taking a closer look. "It's a ring pull from a 1994 can of Fanta, I'd recognize that design anywhere!

My collection is almost complete." Billy had decided that even if he didn't find a stack of gold, there was no way his historical ring-pull collection wasn't going to fetch a small fortune at auction.

"This is the best day ever—"

Rrrrreeeeeeewweeeewwwiiiiiii

The end of Billy's sentence was overtaken by the sound of the metal detector coming to life again. He turned and looked at Bess. Something was wrong. Metal detectors don't start working on their own when they're not moving, either they're on top of metal, or they're not. There was another loud squeak from a bottom.

"Sorry," Billy said to the dog. "I'm just a little nervous." He put the ring pull in his pocket and looked at the ground beneath Bess. He grabbed the trowel, but just as he was about to dig, the earth moved. Something was under there. Maybe it was a mole. Billy wafted Bess over the mound of grass and, sure enough, she started squealing and wailing. If it was a mole, then it was made of metal. As he continued to wave Bess around, the earth moved again, like whatever was underneath was trying to escape. Billy bent down and touched the soil with his hand. The ground felt warm. He sat back in shock. This end of the garden was permanently in the shade. The ground shouldn't be warm.

At that very second, the air was filled with a piercing sound. It wasn't Bess, it was Shakespeare, wincing and howling the same way he did just before a thunderstorm. Billy felt a shiver ripple up and down his spine.

"What's going on? This is no ring pull and that's for sure," Billy said under his breath and leant forward. A small hole in the ground was opening in front of him. Billy glimpsed a beautiful golden crown for a second before it disappeared again. He reached into the soil, grabbed hold of the crown and pulled with all his might, but it was like someone was pulling back from the other side.

"Oh no, you don't!" Billy yelled. "If there's a magic crown to be found, I'm not going to lose it in a game of tug-of-war!" He pulled with all his heart and all his arms until it felt like they might come out of their sockets.

"ONE ... TWO ... THREE!"

Billy cried out and, on three, he flew backwards as a huge flash of orange light filled every inch of the bottom of the garden. It was blindingly bright, but only for a few seconds and then it disappeared. Billy lay in the boggy patch, covered in garden slime. He blinked a few times before sitting up, trying to adjust his eyes. It took a few seconds to find it, but there was his prize: a beautiful golden crown.

The diamonds twinkled and sparkled. Billy gasped. His treasure was sat on the top of someone's head. Thick combed-back greying hair, scowling eyes, a flared nose and a furious mouth were slowly rising out of the hole in the ground. Whoever she was, she did not look amused.

3 p.m.

"AAARRRRRRRGGGGGGGGGGG
GGGGGHHHHHHHHHHHHHHHH!"

Billy took a deep breath.

"AAARRRRRRRGGGGGGGGGGG
GGGGGHHHHHHHHHHHHHHHH!"

Billy took another breath. "Yep, I think
that should do it ... who are you and
why are you in my garden? Do you live
underground? Why are you dressed like

41

Queen Victoria and where did you come from, under the ground? I know I've already asked that, but I feel it's quite an important question, so therefore I'm going to ask it twice. I also might do another scream."

"One is going to chop orf your head!" the lady snorted as she dusted the soil from her dress. "Who are you and whot are you doing in *my* ceiling?"

"What ceiling? It's a garden!" Billy said, standing up. "You can't just chop off people's heads. You can't and won't! I have a weapon!" He reached into his backpack and grabbed what he thought was his gardening fork, only to find he'd thrust out an apple.

"This is no time for a picnic," the lady

said, looking around her. "Guards! Have him thrown in the tower! He tried to steal my crown – the cheek of it all."

"What? No, I did not!" Billy yelled.

"SHAKESPEARE, ATTACK HER!"

he shrieked, turning to the dog, who in all the excitement had gone for a wee.

"Goodness, is that a rabbit?"

"No, he just has rather large ears, that's all. He's actually a French bulldog ... wait, why am I explaining this to you? You want to kill me! Look, I didn't steal your crown; it was stuck in the mud."

"Nonsense, one was sitting down, about to enjoy a bowl of piping hot sausages, when everything went a tad orangey and a hand appeared in my ceiling – a newly decorated ceiling, one might add – and tried to grab my crown. You, sir, just tried to overthrow the monarchy, therefore your head will be chopped orf. Now, where are those guards?"

"Wait, you got the orange-light thing too? I thought it was just me. The crown, I swear, came out of the ground – look it's got mud on it, as have you. See that big hole behind you? That's where you appeared from, I promise. Granted, you were also attached to the crown, but, honestly, I've never stolen anything in my life! Please, I need my head. I have a hat collection! All I wanted was to find some treasure." Billy paused. "Who are you really and why are you dressed like Queen Victoria?"

"One is dressed like Queen Victoria, because one *is* Queen Victoria. The question should be: why are you dressed like that?"

Billy looked at himself. He was in

normal clothes, ones that you can buy in any shop – well, apart from the wellies, which were a bit weird. Billy looked at the Queen, then he looked at the ground. Was she joking? It seemed fairly unlikely that she would bury herself in the garden for years, dressed as a dead monarch, just waiting to play a trick on him. Could she be telling the truth? Billy decided there was only one way to find out. He'd just been doing the Victorians in history, so he had a few facts up his sleeve and he was prepared to use them.

"What year is it?" he asked, his eyes narrowing.

"1882," Victoria said without hesitation.

"Who's the Prime Minister?"

"Gladstone … frightful man, always

yakking on about this, that and the other," she answered. So far, she was correct.

"OK, what's your favourite thing to eat?"

"Pies, of all kinds." She in turn narrowed her eyes.

"What's the best present you ever got?"

"Does India count?"

"Hmm, what's your favourite TV show?"

"What's a tee-vee?"

"Drat, you even beat my trick question!" Billy said. "OK, OK, so say you *are* Queen Victoria, how did you get to here, 2019?"

"Well, one does not know what

number your house is," Victoria huffed.

"No, that's the year," Billy said.

"What *are* you talking about? It is 1882! Time cannot go forward ... well, of course it can, but not like this ... can it?"

"I don't know, but somehow you're here ... from the past." Billy shrugged. "Maybe time can go backwards too?"

"One has had enough of this conversation," Victoria shouted.

"TAKE ONE HOME! I ORDER YOU, TAKE ONE BACK!"

"Well, I'm not sure it's that simple..." Billy said, sticking his trowel into the ground and peering into the muddy hole. "Oh dear, what are we going to do?"

"We? *We?!* One did not do this! You

did!" Queen Victoria yelled. "Now, take me home before one chops orf your head oneself!"

"Err, now, don't do anything crazy..." Billy said, as the Queen strode towards him, her face pink and angry. "There's a nice Queen."

"YOU! COME HERE AT ONCE!"

Queen Victoria yelled and started running.

"Argh!" Billy squealed and ran down the path. Victoria, despite her advancing years, and technically being well over one hundred and thirty years old, was fairly sprightly. She hurdled over the boggy bit and dashed past the blackberry bush – her little legs working twice as hard to keep up with him.

Billy bolted through the patio doors, jumped over Nan's legs and ran up the stairs. Shakespeare, thinking this was the best game ever invented, decided to join in as well, and the three of them bounded up the stairs to Billy's bedroom.

There was nowhere else to run, so Billy hid under the bed, hoping that it would all go away – a method that he'd used fairly successfully over the years.

"Whot is this place?!" Queen Victoria bellowed as she burst into the room. "And whot have you done with my beautiful palace?"

"Leave me alone! Get back in your hole!" a muted cry came from under the bed.

"Is one … hiding?"

"No…"

"Is one under the bed?" Victoria said, sticking her head under the frame and coming face-to-face with Billy.

"AAAAAAARRRRRGHHH!"

he yelled again.

"Well, that's not very British, is it? Listen, you rogue, I am Queen of an unstoppable empire – an empire that will live for thousands of years!"

"Hmm, I wouldn't bank on that."

"Whot?"

"Err … nothing."

"Then get up, man! One needs to go home!" Victoria bellowed. "It's a Saturday, which means it's pie for supper, so pull yourself together and get me orf home!"

"You're right." Billy slid out from under his bed and dusted himself off. "I shouldn't be hiding. I need to fix this. I'm the one who dug you up and I need to put you back in the ground again, so to speak. Hang on, what's this?" Billy said, spotting an old comic under the bed.

"I thought I'd lost this ages ago! Well, this is certainly a good day for finding stuff." He smiled at Victoria. Her face didn't flinch.

"Sorry, it's probably not a good time to read *Adventures Through Time and Space*, is it? Wait a second ... this is just what we need!" Billy whooped in delight.

"What are you going to do with it? Roll it up and use it like a hammer to thwack one back into the ground?" the Queen snapped.

"No, it's just an old comic book, but look at the front." Billy pointed at the cover. "Look at the picture!"

Queen Victoria scowled at it, then

her eyes lit up. There was a spaceman climbing through a hole in the ground, with light pouring out of it.

"Does it remind you of our situation at all?" Billy asked.

"Yes, but this is a work of fiction. How can it help?"

"It is fiction, but the science is real," Billy said, smiling. "It's a wormhole!"

"A wormhole?" Victoria snorted. "One's empire is down a wormhole? That will never do!"

4 p.m.

"Whot is that?" Victoria asked, looking at the strange contraption on Billy's desk.

"It's a computer, for research – all good plans start with a good Google."

"Well, for goodness' sake, nip orf to the lavatory and have a good Google in private!"

"No, a Google is something else. I just need to press..."

"Oh, whot is that?"

"It's a button that turns on the computer," Billy replied.

"Whot is that?"

"It's a mouse—"

"A MOUSE! ARGH!"

"No no no, don't hit it with my cricket bat! It's not that kind of mouse."

"Oh, how many sorts of mice are there?"

"There are ones for computers and, err … all the others."

"Whot is a computer again?"

"Right!" Billy snapped. "I realize that you're from another dimension and this is completely mind-blowing for you, but I can't explain everything just now. This, in case you hadn't noticed, is an emergency and I'm doing my best. I need to look something up on this machine, which is like the world's biggest library, and I make it work with a button and a plastic mouse. Now, if it's OK with you, I need to get on," Billy said, firing up the computer.

"Well, there's no need to be rude …

I am your Queen awfter all." Victoria sniffed, perching herself on the end of the bed and sitting on her hands like a scolded child.

"Well, technically, you're not – we have a different one in this time zone," Billy said, still tapping away on the keyboard.

"Oh, really? Well, one does not want to be Queen of this time zone. Mice are treated better than monarchs! Nothing makes sense. I mean, what even is this supposed to be?!" Victoria said, holding up a big pink piece of rubber.

"It's a whoopee cushion," Billy said mid-Google.

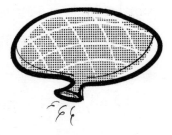

"Whot does it do?"

"Well, you blow in it and then sit down on it."

"Why?" the Queen said, blowing it up.

"You'll see..."

Queen Victoria, with her newly pumped-up cushion, placed it on the edge of the bed and gently lowered herself down onto it.

BRRrrRRRRRrrrrrrRRRRRRR!

The sound of a comedy fart filled Billy's bedroom.

There was a moment of silence.

"That sounds like a...?"

"I know," Billy said. "That's the point."

"My goodness ... how horrid!" She paused. "One is going to do it again."

BRRrrRRRRRrrrrrrRRRRRRR!

There was another moment of silence before the distant rumble of laughter began in Queen Victoria's belly. "BHAHAHAHAHAHA!" she cackled. "Oh, this is marvellous! It reminds me of my Albert after a pork-pie session. How wonderfully silly."

"Aha! I've found it!" Billy said, having finally landed on the right bit of research. "Wormholes," he said, showing Queen Victoria the computer screen, "are like helter-skelters—"

BRRaaaaAAAaaAA!

The sound of a whoopee-ed fart vibrated out once more.

"Terribly sorry," Victoria said, putting the whoopee cushion down.

"Wormholes are like helter-skelters through time and space," Billy carried on, "so you could fall down one hole in one place and end up in another place in space and time. Err, then it mentions a lot of maths and science stuff that I don't really get. What else ... oh yes, it says that while wormholes are real, no one has ever seen one in real life. Wow, that's exciting! I wonder how one ended up at the bottom of my garden? Anyway, it says that once one has opened, it may well keep getting bigger and bigger ... that's a bit annoying."

"So whot do we do now? Can you ask the mouse to go and fetch information on how to close the wormhole?" Victoria asked.

"Yes, well, I don't think that's going to happen. No one has ever seen a wormhole in real life; they've just written about them," Billy said, scanning the screen.

"Like pixies?" Victoria smiled.

"Sort of like pixies, but imagine if pixies could travel through space and time."

"Oh, so not really like pixies at all then?"

"No, not really."

Woof! Woof! Woof! Shakespeare suddenly barked.

"What is it, boy?" Billy said, looking at Shakespeare as he sniffed and barked at the window. Billy ran over and pulled back the curtain. "Uh-oh." He sighed, taking a deep breath.

"Whot is it?" Victoria asked.

"The orange light … it's back," Billy said, staring down at the bottom of the garden.

"Oh, how terribly exciting! I wonder who's popping in for tea now?" Queen Victoria said.

5 p.m.

"Does this woman ever wake up?" Victoria asked, as she, Billy and Shakespeare hot-footed it back through the living room.

"Nan? No, not really. She has her TV, the big box thingy," Billy said, pointing at the *Antiques Roadshow*, "and so long as it's switched on, she stays sound asleep."

Victoria gazed at Windsor Castle on the TV. "Get out of my house!" she cried at the top of her voice.

"THOSE INTERLOPERS ARE IN ONE'S HOUSE, LOOKING AT ONE'S STUFF!"

"Would Your Majesty please shut up!" Billy said. "Later. I'll explain later—"

Suddenly there was a loud wail and a thumping sound in the garden. Billy and Victoria looked at each other and scampered through the patio doors, back towards the hole where Victoria had popped out. They squeezed past the bush, just in time to see a small legion of Roman soldiers fly out of the ground, as if they'd just come down a bumpy slide at a local fair.

WhaaaAAAaa!

Wha!

They yelled
in turn as, one by one,
the soldiers flew out of
the hole, landing in a heap on
top of each other until they were
stacked like a pile of pancakes.

"One ... two ... three ... four ... five,"
Billy counted and sighed. "I guess it
doesn't matter whether I'm sending one

Whaha!

person back through space and time, or six. Hello!" he cried out, speaking slowly like he did when he tried to talk to the locals on holiday. "I don't suppose you're all on your way to a fancy-dress party or this is all part of a huge joke that you're playing on me?"

"Why are you speaking the English? Where are you from? Where are we? Who's that lady? What's happened?" A volley of questions came from the top of the pile of pancakes.

"Tell me, were you looking down a hole when things got a bit ... weirdsy?" Billy asked.

"I do not understand this word 'weirdsy'," answered a man dressed in full Roman centurion clothing. "But yes, one moment we were in battle formation; the next, we were falling. I am Atticus, leader of my men, centurion in the Roman Empire – the greatest empire in the history of the world!"

"Whot now?" Victoria piped up.

"You all speak English?" Billy asked.

"I do. The other lads, not so much," Atticus said, lowering himself down from the pile of soldiers and straightening out his helmet. "I was stationed in England for a year as leader of the road-building division. It was very hard work, all those curvy roads took a long time to build and caused many accidents."

"You should have tried building straight ones," Billy said, thinking out loud.

"Well, that is a good idea," Atticus said. "I might mention it to the boss, Caesar – although he seems to have gone a bit quiet lately—"

"Excuse one," Victoria interrupted. "You were saying something about the Roman Empire?"

"Yes ... the greatest empire in the world," Atticus said, pointing to the stack of dishevelled soldiers.

"TAKE THAT BACK, YOU SCOUNDREL!"

Victoria cried, rolling up her sleeves.

"Otherwise, I'll give you whot for!"

"Well, I think we're getting slightly off topic," Billy said, trying to keep the peace.

"Bring it on indeed, lady! Who are you and what business is this of yours? Women know nothing about what it takes to build an empire…"

"ORF WITH YOUR HEAD!"

Victoria screamed, lurching straight for Atticus's throat with her tiny but pointy hands.

"Right, now who wants to go first?" Billy said in his firm teacher voice, a voice normally reserved for when Shakespeare had stolen his slippers to do something unspeakable to them behind the big chair in the living room. "I can wait all day, you know. I don't have to be anywhere ... I'm happy in this dimension." He drummed his fingers on the dining-room table.

"It just feels weirdsy to say 'I am sorry'. I mean, one is a Queen," Victoria said, looking down at her feet and avoiding eye contact with Billy and the mildly duffed-up Roman soldiers.

"Violence is never the answer," Billy said, looking at Atticus.

"Well, we pretty much hope that

violence is the answer. Otherwise, we're all out of a job!" Atticus chuckled.

Billy raised an eyebrow, his not-to-be-messed-with eyebrow. "If you fight as badly as you build roads, then you might well be," he snapped.

"Fair point... Maybe if the Queen says she's sorry, then we can promise to not get too violent – even though, actually, if anyone's the mean one around here, it's her," Atticus said under his breath.

"I'm ... sorry?" Queen Victoria said, trying her best to do as she was told.

"It would be helpful if you didn't say it as a question." Billy sighed.

"I'm sorry..." the Queen murmured.

"No, say it so we can actually hear it." Billy tutted.

"I'M SORRY!"

Victoria finally cried. "One didn't mean to beat you all up. It's just that empires are very personal things."

"That's OK. We're sorry for..." Atticus started.

"Teasing you," Billy said, helping out.

"Yes, for teasing you. We also realize that we should all be a bit more grateful to Billy, who's doing his level best to try and help us all," Atticus finished. There was a murmuring of agreement from the rest of the soldiers.

"Very good and because you've all learnt a life lesson, you can have some orange squash and a snack and maybe watch a bit of the magic box for a few minutes, while I try and work out what to do. And remember what we said?" Billy asked, looking at everyone.

"MR SHOUTY IS NOT WELCOME IN THE GARDEN,"

they all chanted back to Billy.

"That's right, because Mr Shouty may

well alert the neighbours, and that would be bad, wouldn't it, because then who might come round?" Billy asked again.

"Mr Policeman," everyone said.

"Exactly!" Billy smiled. "I realize that you probably don't know what one of those is, but trust me, in this dimension, they're bad news. Right, someone help me with the KitKats."

Far away, beyond the city, in a darkened room, in a secret bunker under a mountain, an important discussion was taking place between a crack team of scientists.

"Should we go Chunky, or traditional?" Professor Jones asked her colleague as she adjusted her enormous glasses.

"Well, both varieties of KitKat are good, but for dunking purposes, it has to be Chunky every time."

"Dunking?" another person joined in.

"We've been over this, Marjory. Dunking isn't wrong. It's a perfectly acceptable way to behave around chocolate and hot beverages."

"Well, I think you're mistaken, Dave—"

"Err, guys?" another voice interrupted.

"Not now, Derek. Can't you see we're in the middle of something important?!" Professor Jones snapped.

"Yes, but—"

"Very well, Derek. Where do you stand on dunking?" Professor Jones asked. "You can say – there'll be no reprisals. We have Marjory and Dave on very different sides of the argument here and I'm undecided."

"Well, I suppose … no wait, I don't care!" Derek said, changing his mind. "I have something really important to tell you!"

"FOR GOODNESS' SAKE, WHAT?"

Professor Jones shouted.

"You know why we're all here?" Derek began.

"Yes…" the other scientists replied in unison. "To find proof of inter-dimensional travel," they all repeated, parrot fashion.

"Well, I think I have it!" Derek said, waving a piece of paper at them. "Look at this printout from the computer!"

"This isn't like the time you thought you'd found proof of life on another planet, but it turned out to be a sneeze on the chart, is it? Do you remember, Derek? We had to have words, serious words," Professor Jones said sternly.

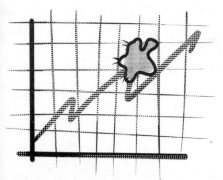

"This ain't no sneeze," Derek said

seriously, showing the Professor the printout.

"You know we're not in an American film, don't you? There's no need to say 'ain't'. Have you been bingeing on Netflix again?"

"Sorry, Professor Jones," Derek said self-consciously. "Anyway, something's wrong – there's been a shift in the cosmos ... a wobble in time!"

"And are you sure it's not the toilet? When someone does a big flush, it makes the whole place shake. I don't want to go to the Prime Minister claiming we've unlocked the secret to inter-dimensional travel, when all it is is Dave trying to flush a big one after too many eggs for breakfast. Not again..."

"I SAID I'M SORRY..."

came a sad voice from the back of the room.

"No, look!" Derek said, pointing to the numbers.

"My goodness!" Professor Jones yelped, standing up and knocking the KitKats off the plate. "This is unheard of! Why didn't you show me this earlier?" she said, looking at the printout, littered with readings that were off the charts. "This may be the greatest discovery since the—"

"KitKat Chunky?" Marjory offered.

"Well, let's not go bonkers ... but it's certainly up there. If this is correct, it looks like a wormhole – a way to travel between the future, past or even to other galaxies – is real, and it's right here in … uh … Clapham. To the science-mobile so we can get there before anyone else finds it!" Professor Jones squealed with delight. "I have spent my life trying to prove the impossible, waiting for the day I can claim my Nobel Prize. Nothing is going to stop us now!"

"Actually, we had to sell the science-mobile so we could afford the coffee machine," Derek added.

"Oh, yes, of course. Well, to the Number Thirty-Five bus then and ring every TV station in the world on the way. This is going to shake the earth to the very core!"

6 p.m.

"So, talk one through this again?" Victoria said in utter shock.

"Well, it's very simple. You put the bread in here, pull this lever and wait for it ... wait for it ... and – *POP!* – you have toast." Billy beamed. He felt like he was showing cavemen fire for the first time.

"One will not lie to you, that has utterly blown one's mind, and I am Queen, so I've seen a lot of wacky stuff. And whot does one call this tin of wonder? Is it called a Victoria? Most things are these days. One can barely get through a day without something being named after me: waterfalls, cakes … bits of Australia."

"No, it's called a toaster, on account of it making toast." Billy grinned.

"This is the most incredible thing I've ever seen." Atticus gasped. "I mean, I didn't even know what toast was until a few minutes ago, but I'm fairly certain it should be worshipped as a god. We have a god for most things these days – love, war, victory … more war – why not one for hot bread?" The other soldiers grunted in agreement.

Billy's plan had worked perfectly; everyone was so distracted making toast that he could now get on with the business of figuring out how to fix the wormhole. He picked up the landline and dialled.

"Hello? Yes, is this Pete the Reliable Plumber? Great! I have a leak, well, it's more of a hole than a leak, but things are definitely leaking out of it – not water so much, but historical figures mainly … no, you heard me right … no, it's in the garden … hello? Are you still there?" Billy put down the phone. "Oh great, well that's just perfect. You, Pete, are about to get a savage review on Trusted Tradesman dot com."

He turned to Shakespeare, who gazed up at him obediently. "I'm running out of ideas, boy, so here goes nothing."

Billy, followed by Shakespeare, marched straight past the toast factory in the kitchen, past a sleeping Nan, towards the bottom of the garden – grabbing the bin lid as he went – past the big spiky bush and, with one swift movement, slammed the dustbin lid down over the hole.

"Right, let that be an end to it!" Billy shouted. "No more Queens, or soldiers, please, wormhole. I command you to leave me in peace!" There were a few seconds of silence. Billy sighed with relief. Then there was a rumble and, slowly, the familiar orange beam began to spill out from under the lid. Shakespeare started to whimper.

"Oh, perfect!" Billy mumbled, edging away from the wormhole. There was a crack of thunder and the sound of metal being punched as the dustbin lid flew off and a huge flash of orange light filled the sky. Maybe he'd made the wormhole angry – could wormholes get angry?

Then the light disappeared again and Billy could make out the figure of a lone man walking slowly towards him, like a gunslinger from an old Western, ready to take down the sheriff.

"PLEASE, PLEASE DON'T HURT ME!"

Billy cried. "I'm really sorry about the bin lid thing!" He decided that now was probably a good time to do some running, but it can be hard to run away when you're wearing over-sized wellies.

"These stupid things!" Billy yelled as he struggled in the mud.

"Hey, you!" a voice boomed from behind him.

"AAAAAARGH!"

Billy screamed.

"Are you all right?" the figure asked in a friendly voice and extended his arm towards him. "Those are ridiculous shoes for a person your age; the ratio is all out of whack, you silly noodlehead!"

Billy turned around and took a good look at the person staring back at him. "It's … it's you!" he said, laughing. "You're you! This is fantastic!"

"Everyone! Everyone! Can I have your attention, please?" Billy yelled as he came back into the kitchen.

"STOP PLAYING WITH THAT STUPID TOASTER!"

Billy bellowed. Any pretence of keeping quiet for Nan had all but gone out of the window. Frankly, Billy had bigger inter-dimensional fish to fry.

"Take that back!" Atticus said, pulling out his sword. "The toaster is not stupid!"

"Oh, do give it a rest, dear," Victoria said, pushing Atticus's sword down. "It's Billy's toaster. If anything, you should be worshipping him. I, on the other hand, have decided to make lunch. Who wants toast and marmalade? It's awfully good, and one has had seventeen slices so far. I'm seeing if one can power on through to twenty-five rounds."

"Yes, well done," Billy said. "Anyway, I've got someone else I'd like you all to meet."

"Oh, goody! Another time tourist. Who have we got now?" Victoria asked.

"Einstein!" Billy grinned.

"Never heard of him. Would you like a slice of toast, Mr Einstein? One has rather run out of bread, so one is using something called Weetabix now. It's harder to get in, but it's totally worth the effort."

"My name is Atticus," the Roman centurion interjected. "I am a soldier to Caesar, a husband to Mary, a worshipper of the God of Toast."

"Yes, yes, do put a sock in it..." The Queen sighed, rolling her eyes.

"HICCCUUUUUUUUUP!"

she belched. "Oh, golly, one feels very strange."

"*Einstein*," Billy said, trying his best to emphasize the name, "is a genius."

"Is he?"

"Am I?" Einstein responded.

"Yes!" Billy said. "Well, if you're not yet, you soon will be."

"OK. Well, that's groovy." Einstein smiled. "So, who wants to tell me what's going on and why and how I'm here?" he continued, pulling a pen and notebook out of his jacket pocket, ready to take notes.

"Not a problem," Billy said. "I'll put the kettle on and then you can figure out how to get everyone home."

7 p.m.

"Aren't we going to look a bit weird?" Derek asked. "I mean, a group of scientists all catching the bus, in full protective suits, carrying portable laser guns?"

"They are not guns!" Professor Jones snapped. "They are very sophisticated laser expulsion units."

"What are the lasers for?"

"To shoot anything scary that comes out of the wormhole. It could be an alien race; it could be the Loch Ness Monster; it could be Jeremy Clarkson – who knows what horrors may be out there!"

"So they *are* guns?" Marjory asked.

"They're science guns!" Professor Jones mumbled. "It's *not* the same."

"Are they legal?" Dave asked.

"Legal-ish." Professor Jones shrugged.

"Look, I must say that this isn't the response I was hoping for. We are the only four people in the world who are trained to deal with what happens if inter-dimensional travel is discovered. We are on the front line of science. We are warriors and, if needs be, defenders of this planet. What did you think this job was about when you signed up for it?" the Professor said, looking around at her colleagues.

"Well…" Marjory began.

"I just thought…" Derek started.

"Yeah, me too…" Dave agreed.

"WHAT?!" Jones barked.

"Well, we didn't ever expect to find anything … I just wanted a quiet life – you know, away from real work."

"Real work?" Professor Jones said, unable to comprehend what she was hearing. "Let me get this straight. Does anyone care about time travel, or did you all take this job because you wanted a quiet life?"

There was silence.

"None of you thought that time travel really existed, did you?"

"I did!" Derek said. "I thought it was real, but then it turned out to be a giant sneeze..." He trailed off.

"Well, this is very disappointing. All those years we spent looking for anomalies in space and time and you lot were just phoning it in." Professor Jones's shoulders slumped in sadness.

"Yeah, but we believe in it now,"

Marjory said. It was hard to see her smile from behind the protective suit.

"You're just saying that to cheer me up," Professor Jones whimpered.

"No, it's true! I mean, we were a little sceptical at first, but we all believe you now," Dave added.

"We're all super excited about our mission," Derek said, offering his support. "Thanks for the guns, Professor. They're well cool."

"Science guns," Professor Jones added. "And you're welcome. Now, do we have the coordinates of where we're going?" she asked her team. They all nodded back at her. "Great! Here comes the bus," she said, sticking out her hand. The crack team of scientists slowly shuffled on board.

"Now, where did I put my Oyster card?" Professor Jones mumbled. "The trouble with protective suits is that once they're on, it's difficult to get to my purse," the Professor said to the driver as she tried to find the right zip.

The driver looked up from the wheel to see four faceless bright white suits holding enormous space guns crowding around him and had a teeny tiny panic.

"YOU CAN GO FOR FREE! JUST DON'T SHOOT ME!"

the driver cried as he tried to climb out of the window.

"Oh no, this isn't a gun! It's a laser expulsion device. Look, it doesn't even fire real bullets," Professor Jones said, accidentally pulling the trigger.

"So, basically, that's the long and short of it. I found a wormhole and you fell through it. Here, take a seat, won't you?" Billy smiled at Einstein. "Stop me if this is getting too technical for you."

"This is amazing!" Einstein laughed and sat down.

BRRRRAAaaaAAAaaA!

A huge farting sound bellowed out from under Einstein.

 "I'm so very sorry," Victoria said, doubled over with laughter. "One just thought we could all do with a chuckle. So sorry. Do carry on."

Einstein cleared his throat. "As I was saying, this is amazing. It may well mean the end of the world and probably the universe as we know it, but, apart from that, this is truly an astonishing discovery. You have proven the unprovable. You've rewritten the entire history of everything. Nothing will ever be the same again."

"Yay me?" Billy said, doing a very small fist bump. "I'm interested in something you said a second ago, all that stuff about the end of the world. What does that mean? Give it to me in simple terms…"

"Well, to put it another way … imagine a vacuum cleaner—"

"I'm going to stop you there, Albert. Most people in the room don't know what that is, but fortunately I have one to demonstrate," Billy said, nipping to the understairs cupboard.

"Is the noise going to wake the old lady?" Einstein asked, craning his neck to check for any movement in the living room.

"I think we'll be all right. The end of the world could actually happen and Nan would probably sleep through it. Just as long as the TV is on, we'll be fine," Billy said.

"OK," Einstein said, grabbing the vaccum cleaner and turning it on. "I need something I can suck up," he said, looking around.

"Oh, hang on," Billy said, grabbing Queen Victoria by the shoulders and giving her a little shake. "Sorry, Your Majesty," he apologized as crumbs rained down from her toast binge.

"So, we have the wormhole and things have been falling through it, yes?" Einstein asked.

Everyone nodded.

"This is like the vacuum cleaner. Everything is being sucked into it,"

Einstein said, hoovering up the crumbs. "But, a wormhole gets bigger and more powerful all the time, so it would be like this vacuum cleaner but – how you say? – the nozzle getting bigger and stronger. The vacuum would start to pull up the carpet, then the furniture and eventually it would eat..."

"Itself..." Victoria said.

"Exactly! Gold star to the Queen. A wormhole will eventually destroy itself and, in doing so, the world would be sucked into a never-ending loop of destruction, where every single atom would explode with the power of a nuclear bomb."

"Okey-dokey ... so a bin lid isn't going to cut it then?" Billy said, clarifying things. At that very second the room started to shake, slowly at first, but building all the time.

"QUICK! EVERYONE HIT THE GROUND!"

Einstein yelled as the toaster rattled uncontrollably on the kitchen counter. Shakespeare bolted out of the kitchen to the living-room window and started barking furiously. Billy crawled along the floor, past a still-sleeping Nan, and stared out into the garden. A swirling tornado of orange light danced round and round between the hedges just beyond the blackberry bush. There was a clap of thunder, the clouds began to bubble and the sky turned a menacing purple colour, as if the sun was being stolen from it. Then there was a terrifying crash and a roar from the bottom of the garden.

"Is this it? Is this the end of the world?" Billy whimpered.

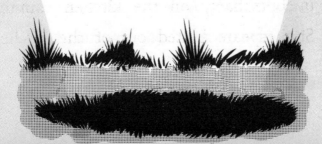

8 p.m.

"Nope, not the
end of the world …
it's just a dinosaur. Well,
actually it's half a dinosaur,"
Billy said, peering out of the
window. There in the garden, a
Diplodocus's neck was sprouting
out of the ground like a palm tree.
"Crikey Mikey with a side helping
of wowzers," Billy muttered.

"Ah, yes ... a Diplodocus," Einstein said, joining Billy by the window. "No need to panic."

"Righto," Billy said. "I'm sorry, but I'm not really sure what to say to that—"

At that moment, the phone rang. Everyone stopped dead in their tracks, especially those who'd never heard a phone ring before.

"WE'RE UNDER ATTACK! THE SAXONS ARE COMING!"

Atticus bellowed, pulling out his sword as he ran into the living room.

"No, we're not! Someone is calling us! Can you stop being so violent. Now, where's the phone? Where's the phone?!" Billy panicked as he looked at the blank faces of the Roman soldiers.

"Whot does it look like?" the Queen asked, pushing past the soldiers.

"Black with buttons!" Billy said.

"This?" Atticus asked, grabbing the TV remote and pushing all of the buttons.

"NOOOOOOOOOOOOO!"

Billy cried, but it was too late. Atticus had pressed the off button for the TV. With no *Antiques Roadshow* in the background, Nan began to stir.

"Argh! If she wakes up, this is going to get worse and I can't deal with worse!" Billy said as quietly as he could, finally finding the phone and clamping his hand over it to block out the ringing sound. He snatched the remote from Atticus and frantically pushed down on the buttons. "It's not working! What do I do? WHAT DO I DO?"

"Make the voice," Victoria whispered to Billy.

"What?" Billy whispered back.

"You know, the voice of the man on the tee-vee? If you make his voice, then she won't wake up," she suggested.

"OK ... that's a good idea ... but *you* need to answer this phone," Billy said.

"Whot?" Victoria asked.

"You need to pretend to be Nan so that I can be the TV man," Billy said, quickly explaining it as best he could.

"Whot does she sound like?!" Victoria asked.

"An old woman, like you, but not as posh," Billy said.

"Well, that's charming," Victoria snapped as Nan's eyes started to open.

"JUST DO IT!"

Billy said, pushing the button on the phone and handing it to Victoria. He quickly stepped in front of the TV and started to speak in the best accent he could to try and lull Nan back to sleep. "I'm looking at a very saggy piece that needs a few repairs—"

"What?" Victoria hissed. "Well, I'm

looking at a rogue who's going to get a smack in the chops!"

"I'm pretending to be the antiques expert! Now, speak into the phone!" Billy said before continuing. "This is worth forty-seven thousand pounds! Well done, I'd sell it right away and go and spend all the money on pizzas!" He looked over at Nan, who had gone back to sleep with a big grin on her face. Billy reached around the back of the TV and switched it back on.

ZZZZZ

"Oh, I see! Terribly sorry, Billy," Victoria said down the phone.

"Hello? Mum?" Billy's mum said from the other end of the line.

"Yes, this is one." Victoria shrugged.

"Is everything OK? Your voice sounds different…"

"Different, you say…" Victoria said, looking confused.

"Yes, you sound like Dame Judi Dench from TV," Mum replied.

"It's too posh!" Billy said. "Make your voice more common. You know, like you're not royalty."

"Oh ... sorry about that. I've just been having a Google," Victoria said into the phone. Billy gave her a thumbs-up.

"Oh, OK..." Mum replied. "How is Billy? He didn't try and put that antiques programme on so that he could get up to mischief, did he?"

"No! There's definitely been no mischief here. Just some toast ... and we've been looking at vacuum cleaners," Victoria said, running out of things to say. "I also like whoopee cushions and magic boxes."

"Oh, right … that's good, I suppose. Look, the weather's pretty bad here. There's been some thunder and lightning and apparently a bus caught fire too, so I think the traffic's bad. We're going to have dinner here and wait until it clears. Is that all right? Would you mind sorting out tea for you and Billy? There's plenty of bread for toast."

"That's fine. You take as long as you need," Victoria said as Billy did some happy jumping with his thumbs up.

"MAYBE DON'T COME BACK AT ALL! BYEEEEEE!"

Victoria shouted and, deciding that this was the end of the conversation, handed the phone back to Billy.

"What was that?!" Billy asked, looking at her furiously. "Don't come back at all?!"

"Excuse me, one is not used to talking on the telephone. I have a little man for that!" Victoria said. "You can't expect one to make things up as one goes along! I'm the Queen, not..." She paused, trying to make something up. "You see, I told you. I don't speak to people unless it's been written down for me, so you can look at me all you like, but it won't change a thing."

"Uh, Billy," Einstein interrupted and pointed out of the window. "I think we've got more pressing things to deal with, don't you?"

"Oh yeah," Billy said, remembering the dinosaur in the back garden. "And it looks like he's brought a friend..."

The Diplodocus's head swayed as the creature growled and snarled at its new surroundings. Its neck was thick like a tree trunk, and almost as tall as the house. On top of its neck sat a tiny little head, snapping and yapping away, and on top of that sat something else.

"WHAT LIGHT FROM YONDER GREAT BIG BLOOMIN' HOLE BREAKS?"

a voice cried out.

Billy rubbed his eyes. "Is that...?"

"Err..." Einstein added.

"OMG! That means one's most gobsmacked," Victoria pointed out. "It's him, *Shakespeare*! I love him. He's so..."

"Talented?" Billy suggested.

"Clever?" Einstein put forward.

"Yummy!" Victoria gushed.

"Well, I didn't expect that," Billy said, raising his eyebrows at Einstein.

"I've seen all of his plays! I used to have his portrait on my wall. That head, it's so..."

"Big?" Einstein said.

"Bald?" Billy added.

"Handsome..." the Queen purred.

"Really?" Billy and Einstein both asked.

"YES!" Victoria snapped.

"Wow! Anyway, we should probably get him down," Billy said, noticing that William Shakespeare was wobbling around uncomfortably on the top of the dinosaur's head. "Are you OK up there?" Billy yelled.

"No! Not really!" came a distant reply, as Shakespeare rode around the garden, thirty metres up in the air. "I'm having a really bad day. Firstly, I was stuck writing my play, then I lost my quill, and finally, I landed on this monster from yonder hole over there."

"Oh yes. One can see how that would really niggle," Victoria said and turned to the others. "We have to save him.

He's very fine – I mean – a very fine playwright! We need to keep his spirits up. Oh, I know something that'll cheer him up!"

"No!" Billy snapped. "No more whoopee-ing!"

"Spoilsport … so what *are* we going to do?" Victoria asked. "I think we need a plan. This sort of thing is likely to draw attention."

"The Queen makes a good point," Einstein said. "I mean, I'm no expert, but people may notice a giant lizard in your garden."

"Well, you do see some strange sights in Clapham, but yes, you're probably right," Billy said.

"That's not the only problem," Einstein

joined in, scratching his head. "The wormhole must be getting more unstable. It's sucking up people and creatures from different times and spitting them out in one go. We need to do something before it rips the universe apart!"

"Right, I'll put that on my to-do list." Billy turned to face Shakespeare. "I'm going to try and help you get down, Mr Shakespeare. Now, sit up for a second … then maybe lie down…" Billy paused and looked over at his dog, who was eagerly following his instructions. "Oh, great, *this* is the time you start to do as you're told?" he muttered before continuing. "OK, roll over … then slide down the dinosaur's neck." Billy

glanced at the very confused dog. "Yeah, I thought that last one would throw you."

Suddenly, there was a thud as the world-famous playwright landed in a heap in front of everyone.

"Ouch." Einstein winced.

Slowly, Shakespeare got up, shook the grass from his head and yelped in fright as Queen Victoria hugged him.

"Madam … how do you do? Why are you all in such peculiar dress?" he asked, looking around in bewilderment.

"It's a long story," Billy said. "But it started with me accidentally pulling Queen Victoria's crown out of the ground. I thought I'd struck gold, but it turns out that all that glitters is not gold—"

"Oh gosh, that's quite good," Shakespeare said.

"Thanks..." Billy laughed. "Anyway, after that, lots of people started falling through a wormhole, which is like a portal through space and time, and you are now about five hundred years in the future. Here are a few other people from history: a Queen, some Roman soldiers and a very clever man who knows about science. We're just trying to work out what to do next before the world is destroyed by a giant vacuum cleaner ... got it?"

Shakespeare looked at them blankly then promptly began sobbing. "Oh, I don't care anyway! I hope the world is destroyed! I hate my life! I hate writing! I detest *everything!*"

"WHAAAAAAAAT?!"

Victoria, Einstein and Billy all yelled. Atticus and the Roman soldiers were less bothered about Shakespeare and more worried about the giant dinosaur that was trying to nibble the plumes on their helmets.

"But you're really good at writing. Really ace," Billy said. "Listen, Mr Shakespeare, I understand that artistic types sometimes have these little moments – I know it's part of the process – but do you think we could talk about your troubles later on, and in the meantime, see if we can save the world?"

Shakespeare stuck out his lip and nodded slowly. Billy turned to Einstein. "I need your help, big guy. We all loved your vacuum cleaner talk, it was great, but now we need the biggie. How do we solve this? How do we send everyone home and stop the wormhole before we all die? Go, buddy, go!"

"Err … do you have a star?" Einstein asked.

"Nope…" Billy said after thinking for a second. "Righto, a bit disappointing. So I'm guessing that means the end of life as we know it? Who's for putting the kettle on and cracking open the secret chocolate Mum and Dad hide for when I go to bed? I mean, it doesn't matter now, does it?!" Billy took a deep breath. "What would a star do anyway?"

"It has a huge mass ... it's so dense that if we put it in the hole, it would reverse the wormhole."

Billy stopped in his tracks. A smile spread across his face. "I know what to do!" he cried. "I know what to do!"

ROOoooooOAR!

The Diplodocus roared, dropping a tree in the middle of Billy's lawn.

9 p.m.

"Say that again?" the policeman said, looking directly into the bus driver's eyes.

"I told you, a gang of them – probably aliens, but I couldn't be certain – jumped aboard my bus, carrying weapons; laser weapons, like from the future..."

"And then what? Did they try and steal the bus?"

"Oh no, they just said they were scientists on their way to find a – what did they call it? – oh yes, a wormhole."

"A what now?"

"A wormhole. It's like one of those slides you get at the pool, except it doesn't dump you out in the shallow end, but rather in a different place in time and history. I did some Googling."

"And they said that one of those is in ... Clapham?"

"Yep," the bus driver answered.

"Then what happened?"

"Well, then there was a lot of hullabaloo."

"Hullabaloo?"

"Yes, hullabaloo. It's several stages away from mischief. There's mischief, shenanigans, hullabaloo and then I think it's Armageddon. Anyway, they were

129

dressed in spacesuits, causing hullabaloo on my bus, when one of their laser weapons went off." The driver paused and shook some soot from his hair. "The bus caught fire and the aliens all ran away, so I phoned you."

"Well, this is very strange. It sounds like there may be some sort of invasion from another dimension. Either that or there's a perfectly reasonable explanation for all this, but I'd rather not take any chances. As they used to say at police-training camp: if in doubt, lock 'em up, ask questions later. I think I may have to call for back-up. Maybe the Air Force can scramble a few helicopters and get to the bottom of this. Which way did the so-called scientists go?"

"That way, towards that unholy menacing presence."

"Poundland?"

"No, I mean the big purple skies and angry clouds."

"Oh, that would make more sense."

The policeman paused and dialled a number on his phone. "Oh, hello? Yes, is that the Air Force? Great ... I don't suppose you've got a couple of hours and half a dozen helicopters to spare, have you?"

A van screeched to a halt by the burning bus and reporters with cameras and microphones jumped out. "Excuse me, officer, we've had a report of some sort of cosmic event. Can you give us a comment?"

"We may be experiencing an invasion from another dimension, but I really can't comment any further. All I can say is that the army are on standby to defend Planet Earth. And that probably, the best thing is to stay indoors and shut the windows."

Billy ran inside to the living room. He reached into Nan's handbag and pulled out a piece of paper.

"This is our answer to everything!" Billy said triumphantly. "What we have here, friends, Romans and monarchs, is the recipe for the densest material known to man. Let me introduce you to my nan's rock cakes," Billy said, reaching into the bag and pulling one out. "I've seen one of these knock a burglar clean out. It can blunt your teeth in seconds, and it weighs more than a star," Billy said throwing one to Einstein, who nearly fell through the wall trying to catch it.

"My goodness, how is there so much weight to what looks like a normal cake? This is not possible."

"I know, my nan's got mad skills, hasn't she?" Billy smiled. "So, we have the recipe. All we need to do is double, maybe quadruple the ingredients until we have a rock cake the size of a cannonball. Then we can simply drop it down the hole and…"

"The cake will begin to expand," Einstein said, his face lighting up. "The gravitational pull will be so huge that it will reduce the hole to a tiny trickle. It should reverse the process and stop everything flying out … thus saving the world." Einstein clapped. "That, my boy, is brilliant."

"Great, but how will we get home again?" Atticus asked.

"Well, imagine that time is like an elastic band – you can pull and stretch it, but it wants to snap back. If we all jump into the wormhole, we should, in essence, snap back to where we came from. Nothing will change. We will have no memory of this. It'll be like we've never been away – we might just feel a little woozy, like when you stand up too quickly. At least that's the theory anyway."

"Well, if it's good enough for Einstein, then it's good enough for me," Billy said.

Suddenly Shakespeare, the dog, began to bark at the window again. Billy looked out to see the Diplodocus squatting on the grass. "Do not do a big dino turd on my lawn!" he shouted out of the window. "Hold it until you get back to your own dimension! It's a one-thousand-pound fine for dog fouling around here; how much do you think it's going to be for a Diplodocus?" Billy shook his head and turned back to the dog. "Well done, Shakespeare. You really are a good boy."

"Thank you. I try my best, but it's not easy," Shakespeare said and bowed.

"No, not you, the dog, you know ... for alerting me to the dinosaur. This is getting confusing."

"Why is the dog called Shakespeare? It's not a common name."

"Well, actually, he's named after you!" Billy said, trying to cheer him up.

"I've got a waterfall named after me," Queen Victoria whispered in Shakespeare's ear.

"Why did you name the dog after me?"

"Well, we were doing Shakespeare at school, and then we got a dog who basically sleeps and yawns a lot and your play—" Billy stopped, realizing where he was going with this.

"My play what? Made you sleepy too?" Shakespeare said looking horrified.

"No, I didn't say that!"

"You were going to, though! Do children find me ... boring?"

"Look, I think sometimes it's hard to teach kids stuff that's really old."

"Do they talk about us?" Atticus piped up.

"Yes."

"Are we boring?"

"Oh no. Everyone loves the Romans," Billy said. "I mean..."

"Oh, so people like the Romans, do they?" Shakespeare shouted.

"Kids like gory stuff, you know ... blood and guts. The Romans did a lot of that ... but we don't have time for this."

"That's it! I'm giving up on writing; you've just convinced me. If all I can hope for is having a dog named after me, then what is the point? It's no waterfall, is it?"

"Look, please don't do that. It's really important that you keep writing. My mum loves you. She even took Dad to see a play of yours on their first date. You definitely get better."

"BETTER? BETTER?!"

Shakespeare cried. "That's it, I'm not going home. I don't care if it messes with history. I'm staying here to find another job."

"Like what?!" Billy asked.

"I don't know. I'll be that man, he looks happy," Shakespeare said pointing at a newspaper, which was the first thing that came into view.

"You want to be chairman of Marks and Spencer?" Billy said, glancing down at the business section. "I don't think that's a goer. I mean, do you have any retail experience?"

"I DON'T CARE. I'M NOT GOING HOME AND YOU CAN'T MAKE ME!"

And with that, Shakespeare stormed off upstairs.

"Billy," Einstein said. "We need to get everyone back into the wormhole. We all need to be dropped into history exactly where we left off. If one of us is left out, the consequences could be unfathomable, and if someone as important as Shakespeare doesn't go home…"

"My parents might never have gone on a date … I might not be here without him," Billy said, suddenly realizing what was at stake.

"Exactly. No Shakespeare means no you and no plan to fix the wormhole. That means the world will end. If he doesn't go back, we're all doomed. My boy, the fate of the world is in your hands."

10 p.m.

"Right, so I, a schoolboy, have to convince the world's greatest writer to write, even though I've only studied half of one of his plays and that made me yawn?"

Einstein, Victoria and the legion of Romans all nodded back at him.

"That's fine. I mean, why not? Why the heck not?! Let me do that and then we can bake a cake that's going to save the world, all before my parents get home!" Billy shouted. "I'm going to need a big holiday after this – a really big one with drinks served in coconuts." Billy took a deep breath, high-tailed it upstairs and banged on the bathroom door.

"William, hello, is that you? I don't want to be a pain, but we really need to get going to, you know, avoid the end of the world and all that."

"IT ALREADY IS THE END OF THE WORLD!"

Shakespeare wailed.

"Is this because I said your plays were a bit old and I named my dog after you?"

"Yes, unless there are any other insults you'd like to throw my way, you rogue!"

"Look, I really liked learning about you at school. Yes, it was tricky to get into the play, because of the language – there was an awful lot of 'doth' and 'dith'."

"'Dith'? That's not even a word."

"Well, mostly 'doth', which is tricky to understand, especially when you have teachers like Mrs Grice who's old and a bit shouty, but I really got into it."

"Which one was it?"

"*Romeo and Juliet*. It's a classic."

STRATFORD EVENING TELE GRAPH

Romeo & Juliet by william Shakespeer

★ ★ ★

"Really? The *Stratford Evening Telegraph* only gave it three stars. And they spelt my name wrong. A man who juggled turnips in town got five stars!"

"Well, it's a slow-burner but you can't give up! You've had a bad day ... I'm having a bad day too, so what am I doing? I'm fixing it with a really big cake. All you need is a spoonful of imagination, a cup of inspiration..."

"What are you talking about?"

"Sorry, I was going for a whole cake metaphor thing ... it was a bit rubbish."

"It wasn't great. It didn't even have any rhyming couplets."

"I don't know what they are, but then again I'm not a writer. You, however, are! You see, you know what you're talking about. You just need to get started."

"I can't ... I lost my lucky quill!" Shakespeare sobbed. "Without it, I can't even finish the play I'm writing."

"Well, what's it about?"

"Kittens and puppy dogs. It's set in Denmark."

"That sounds ... fun, but remember what I said about the Romans? Kids like all that blood and guts stuff; they like to be scared."

"Do you think I should change it then?"

"Maybe ... why not put a king or a ghost in it?" Billy said. "At least give it a go, please – for my sake, and also all of human kind?"

"OK," Shakespeare finally answered, before unlocking the bathroom door and poking his head out. "Can I borrow a quill?"

"I can do better than that." Billy ran into his room and grabbed his old pencil case and some paper. "How about a pencil? You can write with it and use the rubber on top to rub out any mistakes," Billy said, offering Shakespeare his case. "Now, what would you prefer, a 2B or not 2B?"

"Say that again?" Shakespeare said.

"2B or not 2B? I have loads of different ones," Billy said.

Shakespeare grabbed the pencil and started scribbling away.

"I LOVE IT!" he yelled in delight.

"So, shall we go back downstairs?"

"Of course, old bean." Shakespeare grinned.

"Great! I'll make you some tea," Billy yelled after him.

"Oh, no need. I drank from your delicious water bowl on the floor." Shakespeare beamed.

Billy looked at the toilet and grimaced. He followed Shakespeare back into the kitchen and stood on a chair to address everyone.

"RIGHT, MY PARENTS GET HOME ANY MINUTE, WHICH WILL LITERALLY BE THE END OF THE WORLD, SO WE NEED TO GET A MOVE ON."

"Romans! I need you to guard the wormhole, just in case anything unsavoury comes out of it; I'm talking dictators, tyrants, warlords, basically anyone with silly facial hair. Einstein! How are you at measuring and multiplying?"

Einstein shot Billy a look.

"Probably pretty good, aren't you? I mean, you did come up with $E=MC^2$, so I'm sure you can weigh some plain flour."

"I came up with what? $E=MC^2$? What is that?"

"Oh, has that not happened yet? Well, let's put it this way: it was one of your greatest hits!"

"I may write that down. What does the E stand for?"

"Hmm, it might be something to do with eagles, but I may be making that up … anyway, you measure, Queenie, you mix, Shakespeare, you do the baking."

"WOOF!"

"No, not you. You're on dino-watch duty. Let's go, people! We have a world to save!"

"We make a good team, don't we, William?" Victoria said, getting her whisk out.

"We must be almost there!" Professor Jones said as the team of scientists walked up Billy's street, looking at the menacing clouds that had gathered above his back garden. "It's like the end of the world around here."

"Especially with that bus catching fire and all..." Derek mumbled.

"Now, listen. We're all sad about the bus catching fire – no one more than me – but we have to think of the bigger picture here; the world's greatest scientific discovery. We will pay for the damage once we get our Nobel Prize, once we have become rock stars of the science world, but right now, we have a job to do. Did you call the media?"

"Yeah, *South London Today* said they might take a look if they had time."

"What?"

"Well, it's hard to convince the world of time travel without sounding like you're loopy."

"Anyone else?"

"*Loose Women* said they would pop in too."

Just at that second, there was a huge roar from Billy's garden as the Diplodocus reared right up, like a scene from

Jurassic Park – if *Jurassic Park* had been set on an estate in South London.

"Holy mackerel!" Marjory screamed.

"NO ONE MOVE!"

the police inspector bellowed through a megaphone as half a dozen police cars screeched to a halt in front of the scientists.

"STOP INVADING OUR PLANET! IT'S AGAINST INTERNATIONAL LAWS, AND ALSO, YOU CAN'T SET A BUS ON FIRE HERE EITHER!"

"What?!" Professor Jones yelled, spinning around.

"Watch out! They're armed with space guns!" the inspector cried out.

"WHAT ON EARTH IS GOING ON HERE?"

Mum shouted, getting out of the car just in time to see the Air Force fly over the house and a dinosaur eating the roof.

"Who are you?" the inspector asked.

"This is – was – my house!" Dad said, also getting out of the car.

"Who are you?" Mum replied. "And who are they?" she asked, pointing at Professor Jones and her gang of laser-gun-wielding scientists.

"Aliens!" the police inspector cried. "Or time travellers, or something."

"WHAT? I'M FROM COVENTRY!"

Professor Jones cried back. "We're here to investigate what's happening. I work for the government," she said, putting her hands up.

"Well, I'm lost. What's going on? Does anyone know what's going on?" the inspector shrieked, pointing as the sky grew ever darker and the clouds boiled and bubbled.

Mum and Dad looked at each other. "Billy!"

"Keep pushing!" Billy said, as they all struggled to get the rock cake through the back door.

"It's stuck!" Einstein said, gritting his teeth. "Maybe we should try rolling it back into the house and out of another door."

"Don't look at me. One is still a Queen, you know! One is not used to rolling anything except maybe my *R*s."

"I wish you'd roll your *R*s over here and help!" Billy grunted.

"Why don't you get the Diplodocus to help?" Atticus asked.

Billy's eyes lit up. "That's a great idea!" He squeezed past the others and stuck his head out of the door. "Oh, dino! Please stop eating the roof and come here! Who wants to play ball?" Billy put two fingers in his mouth and whistled. The Diplodocus paused then took another bite of roof tiles. All of a sudden, Shakespeare, the dog, leapt over the rock cake and ran towards the dinosaur, barking furiously at its legs. The Diplodocus's head craned down to the floor, like a giant snake following Shakespeare as he trotted back to the door. The dinosaur sniffed at the giant rock cake and tried to bite it, before wincing in pain.

"We've all been there..." Billy said sympathetically. "Now, go! Put the ball in the hole ... good dino!"

Slowly but surely the Diplodocus picked the cake up in his mouth and pulled it out of the door frame, taking some of the door with him. It must have taken all of his strength but he did it.

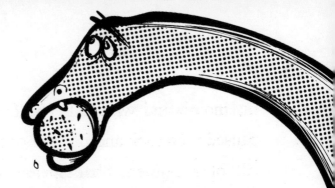

Shakespeare, the dog, followed by the others, guided the dinosaur along, ushering him down the garden towards the wormhole.

"Good boy, Shakespeare!" Billy said. "Almost there!"

"Why, thank you." Shakespeare blushed.

"Not you!" Billy said. "So, what now, Einstein? Does everyone just jump in?"

"Yes!" Einstein shouted.

By now the bottom of the garden was a hurricane of noise and light exploding from the wormhole. Billy edged towards the hole and peered in.

He could see stars and galaxies floating around in it.

"Woah, just in time! It looks like the *Titanic* has just left port!" Billy said, watching the giant vessel float past. "Quick! Put the rock cake in! Then everyone jump back in!"

Just at that second, Mum, Dad, several armed policemen and a crack team of scientists came running up to the garden fence.

"Oh boy, I'm really in trouble now!" Billy shouted, shaking his head.

"It's OK ... all you need to do is get them to go into the wormhole too. That way they'll pop out in a different timeline and they won't remember a thing." Einstein winked.

"Are you absolutely sure? I don't really want to lose my parents in space and time if I can help it."

"Of course I am! The same thing will happen to me and everyone else who's not meant to be here. We won't remember anything once we go back. You must trust me, Billy!"

"OK," Billy said. He whistled at the dinosaur, who took the hint and let go of the giant rock cake. It had an immediate effect. Suddenly the hole started to calm down. It seemed less angry, like it was shrinking.

"We don't have time for long goodbyes! It's now or never!" Billy said, looking over his shoulder at a fast-approaching Mum and Dad.

"Romans, it's been great! Good luck with all that conquering, but please, try and remember to be nice too." Billy snatched a piece of litter from the bush. "Maybe swap conquering for cooking?" he said, handing the soldiers a pizza menu. "I think the locals are going to love it."

"Thank you, Billy!" Atticus smiled, before ordering his troops to jump into the hole.

Billy grabbed a stick and threw it into the hole after them. "Goodbye, dino, we'll miss you!" The Diplodocus leant into the hole before toppling through the portal and back into its own time. Billy turned around and smiled at the Queen. "Right, Victoria, thank you for all your help, it's been a hoot. Have you got everything, your crown?"

"Yes, all here. Toodle-pip, old bean, and thank you. Who knew that doing things oneself could be such fun. Perhaps one has been too grumpy for too long. Maybe I should lighten the mood a little at the palace. Talking of which, here's your whoopee cushion," the Queen said waving it at Billy.

"Why don't you keep it?" Billy beamed. "Just use it wisely. No one likes a serial whoopee-er."

"Thank you, Billy. Goodbye," the Queen said quietly and stepped into the wormhole. "And goodbye, William!" she shouted, batting her eyelashes. And with that, she was gone.

Billy turned to the two remaining time travellers. "Goodbye, Einstein, and thank you for all of your help," he said, holding out his hand.

"You're welcome, Billy – and, just before I go, remind me, what was that $E=MC^2$ you were telling me about?"

"I'm afraid I can't explain it but, just remember, it's all relative." Billy smiled, watching Einstein frantically write something down on his notepad as he disappeared into the hole.

"Will-i-am Shakespeare, the best playwright of all time! Give me a fist bump!" Billy cried.

"What?" Shakespeare answered.

"I don't know really … I just mean, goodbye."

"Oh right. Yes, goodbye and thank you for the pencil. I hope that the next play I write won't make you too sleepy!" He beamed, and, with a jump into the orange light, he was gone.

"WHO ON EARTH WERE THOSE PEOPLE AND WAS THAT A DINOSAUR?!"

Mum screamed as she, Dad, the police inspector and the crack team of scientists pushed past the bush.

"Mum, Dad, strange people in masks and policeman, I can explain. All you

need to do is look into this hole and everything will become clear," Billy said, standing behind the crowd as they edged towards the wormhole. "A little closer, that's it—"

With one finger, Billy pushed his dad's shoulder and, like dominoes, they all fell into the wormhole, just before it closed up completely.

Billy looked over at the old, half-decrepit shed and, with all his might, managed to pull it over the space where the wormhole had been, to keep it safe from prying eyes. Just then, he heard the car door slam from the front of the house. He picked up his beloved Bess and strolled up the garden. The roof was fixed again, like nothing had happened. It couldn't have been eaten by a Diplodocus because, of course, the dinosaur was never here. Billy strolled into the living room and turned off the TV. Nan woke up instantly.

"Oh, did I drop off there for a second, lad?" she asked, looking at her watch.

"Maybe just for a moment." Billy smiled.

"Billy!" Mum called as she and Dad came through the front door. "There's some sort of costume party going on outside. There's a load of confused-looking policemen and people dressed like spacemen walking about! Anyway, sorry we're so late back. How are you both?"

"All good." Billy grinned. "How was shopping?"

"Oh, not too bad, son. I do feel a bit woozy though," Dad said.

"How's the homework going?" Mum asked.

"I've just got a bit to finish off," Billy said. "I'm going to write all about how I met Queen Victoria, Einstein, Shakespeare and some Roman soldiers."

"I thought you hated Shakespeare?" Dad chuckled. "I know I'm not a fan. Remember when you took me to see *Hamlet*, it went on for hours … it was so bleak. He should have put a kitten in it to lighten the mood."

"Well, you can't please everyone." Billy smiled to himself. "And I like Shakespeare, he's a nice fella and he may be many things, but boring isn't one."

"Well, you might be able to use this," Mum said handing Billy a book. "I thought you could do with some inspiration, so I got you a present."

Billy opened the bag. It was a history book. He flicked through it and stumbled on a picture of Queen Victoria. He was sad that she wouldn't remember her time with him, but then he peered at the photo. She was sat with the very same crown on, slyly grinning. And there, a bit blurry and in black and white, was his whoopee cushion.

☆ Get your facts straight! ⚡

See if you know the answers to these questions to fill the gaps in time:

Who was the first Roman Emperor?
1. Julius Caesar
2. Augustus
3. Tiberius

What was Queen Victoria's husband called?
1. Albus
2. Albert
3. Schubert

Which equation did Einstein come up with?
1. $F=MC^4$
2. $E=MC^3$
3. $E=MC^2$

Which language was spoken throughout the Roman Empire?

1. Italian
2. English
3. Latin

Which Queen was on the throne when some of Shakespeare's first plays were performed?

1. Queen Elizabeth I
2. Queen Victoria II
3. Queen Elizabeth II

Answers: Augustus; Albert; E=MC²; Latin; Queen Elizabeth I

Make your own ye olde quill

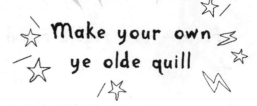

You will need:

- A goose feather
- A pot
- Water
- Food colouring
- Scissors

Directions

1. Carefully snip the end of the stem of the feather at an angle.

2. To make the ink, mix a teaspoon of water with ten drops of food colouring in a pot and stir.

3. Add your quill to the pot and draw up the ink.

4. Get a piece of paper and get writing!